Norbert's Nose

Text by Michele Lee Petrucci and Stephan Schaffrath

Art by Stephan Schaffrath

Norbert doesn't remember much about the beginning, except that it was dark and there was lots of nudging, licking, and crawling.

Sometime later, Norbert's eyes opened and he finally got to see his mommy and his three sisters and two brothers. They all had soft and curly black coats, and their undercoat was amber brown and white. All had white muzzles and white paws.

Norbert's mommy was so beautiful. All dogs in his family were Bernese Mountain Dogs. They were from the Swiss Alps close to the city of Bern.

Norbert's family were working dogs. They specialized in pulling carts through the most difficult mountain terrains. The first day of cart school got off to a bad start for Norbert. He put his cart's harness on backward. It wasn't natural for Norbert, and he had a difficult time.

Even when Norbert figured out how to properly work his cart, he just did not enjoy it. His brothers and sisters loved it, but Norbert would much rather go into the forest and play around in the dirt and leaves.

Norbert loved to dig up dirt taters – at least that's what he called them. No one else in his family cared much about dirt taters. His sisters and brothers even laughed at him. This made Norbert sad, and he would avoid spending time with them.

One day when Norbert was out on his own he met a strange looking Bernese Mountain Dog. He sniffed his new friend and learned that this was no Bernese Mountain Dog, even though his fur markings were just like Norbert's. His new friend, Oskar, was a cat, but Norbert and Oskar joked that Oskar was a Bernese Mountain Cat. They shared the same sense of humor and felt like long lost brothers.

Norbert found out that Oskar looked quite different from his brothers and sisters, and – like Norbert – he also enjoyed going on long walks in the woods. Oskar's brothers and sister preferred to stay home and take long naps in the sun in front of their house.

When Norbert told Oskar about his love for dirt taters, Oskar knew just whom to ask. Rupert, a local truffle pig, knew everything about mushrooms and other edible things found in the woods. “This is no dirt tater,” said Rupert. “This is a beautiful truffle that you found there in the forest, Norbert.” Rupert told his new friends about a famous chef who paid a lot of money for truffles.

So, after talking and planning, Norbert, Oskar, and Rupert decided to go into business together. They were an odd trio, but they liked each other very much.

Norbert and Rupert would find and dig up beautiful truffles, and Oskar made use of his many connections and friendly personality to sell the truffles. Soon, they became famous for their truffles and did very well for themselves. And, they never worried about what others thought.

TRUFFLES

The End

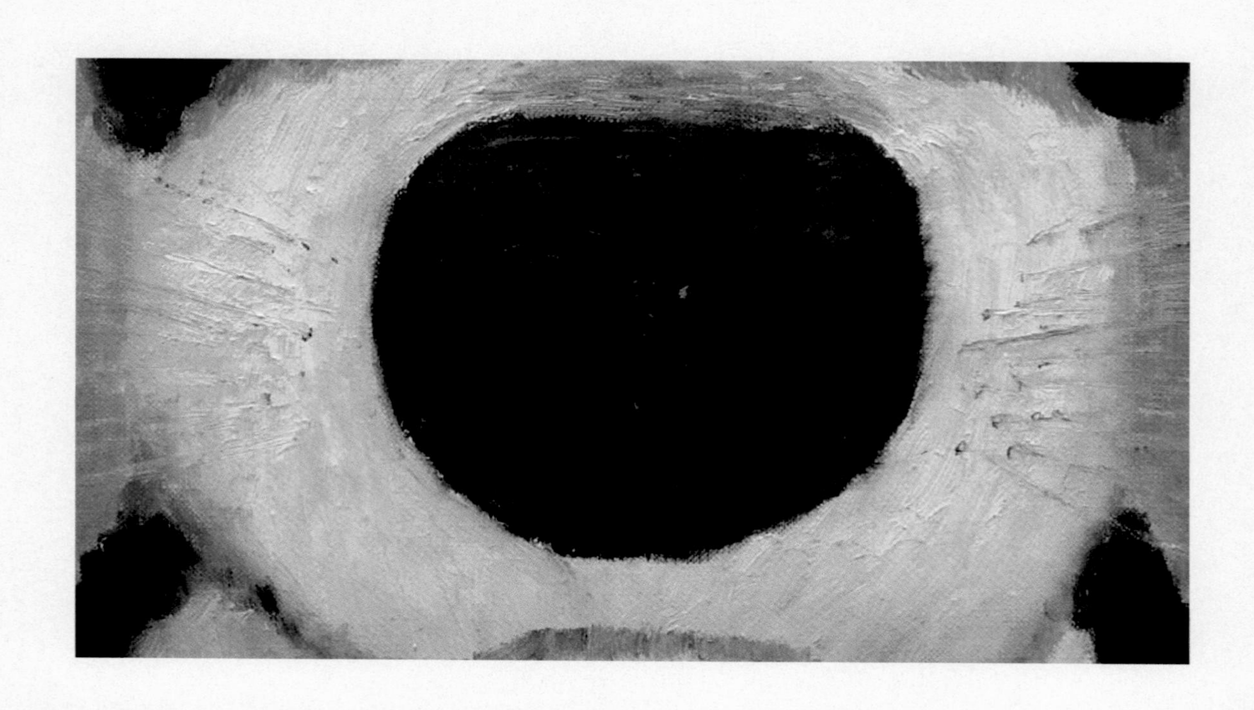

Made in the USA
Lexington, KY
30 April 2019